To our dear Audrey,

This was from our trip to Vail, Colorado
April 21, 2021. We love you!

Grammy & Poppop

Eli and Mort's Epic Adventures Vail

About this project

The idea for Eli and Mort's Epic Adventures Series came from the joy we experienced watching our kids ski, snowboard and have the time of their lives growing up in the Vail Valley. We wanted to share that joy and this beautiful place with the world. We decided to write a series of books through the eyes of a child on an epic adventure. This is the second in the Series, "Eli and Mort's Epic Adventures Vail." The first in the Series is "Eli and Mort's Epic Adventures Beaver Creek."

When considering the concept we imagined what a child might see and feel when they stood at the top of the mountain about to take the first run of the day, and thought, "Who better qualified to illustrate the book than the children that live here?" As a result, we agreed that the background illustrations should be drawn by the children of the Vail Valley.

About the characters

Eli a 5-year-old boy and his pal Mort the Moose are the best of friends exploring the world together. When others are around Mort is a stuffed moose but to Eli, Mort is his "partner in fun." In this book, they are experiencing all that Vail has to offer for children.

Eli and Mort are dedicated to the loves of our lives,
Josh, Heath & Will.

Enjoy!

Created by Elyssa Pallai and Ken Nager
Published by Resort Books Ltd.
Background illustrations by the children of the Vail Valley
Character Illustrations by Eduardo Paj
Background Cover image by Linnea Joy Iverson

Production Date: February 2015
Plant & Location: Printed by Shenzhen Caimei Printing Shenzhen, China
Job/Batch #: 53704-0

Thank you

We love our friends in the Vail Valley. Mort and I think you are AWESOME! Special thanks to Eduardo Paj for making us look so good, Nicole Magistro from the Bookworm who inspired us to write this, Lauren Merrill at Alpine Arts Center, Brent Bingham and PhotoFX and Brenda Himelfarb, Tara Bakos and Diane Pallai for making sure what we wrote was what we meant to write. "Hooray!" to all of the AWESOME children and their parents who illustrated this book and the Education Foundation of Eagle County for their ongoing support in helping us reach the world.

Thank you Vail Resorts. Vail, Epic Pass, and other marks are trademarks of Vail Resorts and used with permission.

Visit **eliandmort.com** to order our latest adventure, check out our events or to just say, "Hi!"

A portion of the proceeds of this book go to the Education Foundation of Eagle County.

The Illustrators

Eli and Mort would like to thank the AMAZING local children, ages 7 to 17, that illustrated the backgrounds! Below are some of their favorite things to do in Vail. What's yours?

Iara Melgarejo
Avon Elementary School
10 years old
Favorite: Ski

Grant Maurer
Berry Creek Middle School
12 years old
Favorite: Ski and snowboard

Addison Maurer
Berry Creek Middle School
10 years old
Favorite: Ski and tubing

Harrison Rubis
Berry Creek Middle School
12 years old
Favorite: Ski and snowboard
Yonder trees on a powder day and go to Fuzzywigs

Kjersti Moritz
Vail Mountain School
10 years old
Favorite: Ski

Ella Smiley
Brush Creek Elementary
7 years old
Favorite: Ski

Kyler Weatherred
Brush Creek Elementary School
7 years old
Favorite: Ski Chaos Canyon

Isabelle Shedd
June Creek Elementary
10 years old
Favorite: Ski double black diamonds

Dylan Berlin Dodds
Stone Creek Charter School
10 years old
Favorite: Ski and after get a surprise that I'm always hoping is ice cream

Eva Thomas
Vail Mountain School
10 years old
Favorite: Ice skate

Linnea Joy Iverson
Home schooled
8 years old
Favorite: Farmer's market

Jesus Guadian
Avon Elementary School
10 years old
Favorite: Snowboard

Jessie James Allen
Vail Christian Academy
7 years old
Favorite: Ski

AnaBel Johnson

Battle Mountain High School
17 years old
Favorite: Ski with friends, farmer's market, Mountain Games, 4th of July parade

Lorenzo Molinar

Berry Creek Middle School
11 years old
Favorite: Go down the mountain and do cool tricks

Mika Leith

Homestake Peak School
12 years old
Favorite: Ski

Taylor Petersen

Battle Mountain High School
17 years old
Favorite: Ski the backbowls

Heath Nager

Brush Creek Elementary School
9 years old
Favorite: Snowboard the terrain park

Caitlyn Weathers

Eagle Valley Middle School
11 years old
Favorite: Snowboard and build snow forts

Cole Maurer

Battle Mountain High School
14 years old
Favorite: Ski

Kendra Loise Hoyt

Vail Ski & Snowboard Academy
14 years old
Favorite: Ski and Fuzzywigs

Liv Moritz

Vail Mountain School
10 years old
Favorite: Figure skating

Sophie Russell

Berry Creek Middle School
11 years old
Favorite: Ski and sled

Gracie Allen

Vail Christian Academy
10 years old
Favorite: Go to Pirate Ship Park

Tommy Johnson

Berry Creek Middle School
12 years old
Favorite: I like to tube, ski, snowboard, snowmobile and have fun

Hannah Litt

Eagle County Charter Academy
13 years old
Favorite: Ski the trees

Madeline Shedd

Battle Mountain High School
14 years old
Favorite: Ski down Lindsey's on the front side of Vail

Anthony Beacon

Berry Creek Middle School
11 years old
Favorite: Skiing and going to the river to skip rocks

Annika Iverson

Home schooled
10 years old
Favorite: Tubing at Adventure Ridge

Leah Ratchford

Eagle Valley Middle School
11 years old
Favorite: Visit my dad while he is at work and ski with my family

Kjersti

A is for **Adventure Ridge**. When my
stepmom, dad, li'l sis, Mort the Moose
and I arrived in Vail it was too late to ski
but Adventure Ridge was open. I drew an S in
the snow for "Start" and, as they pushed Mort
and me down the tubing hill, our adventure in
Vail began!

Isabelle
Shedd

B is for the **Back Bowls** of Vail where snowboarders "catch air" in giant bowls of snow that look like vanilla ice cream. They glide down the mountain's face, leaving licorice trails behind them. My dad told us Vail was famous for its back bowls like Sunup, Sundown and China Bowl.

Linnea Joy Iverson

C is for running through the **Covered Bridge** as we entered Vail Village. Mort and I stopped to throw a snowball in the creek and make a wish. We watched the splash from the snowball and kept our eyes on it as it melted, disappearing into the rushing, icy water. I thought it went all the way to the ocean. So did Mort. But dad told us it flowed into the Eagle River.

D is for **Dog Sledding.** "Mush, Mush," the musher yelled and away the dogs ran. The sound of the dogs barking was so loud we couldn't even hear ourselves laughing. "Whoa! Whoopee!" Mort laughed as he fell off the sled.

E is for rancher **Earl Eaton** and Peter Seibert who decided to build Vail Mountain in 1962. They dreamed of something big and made it come true.

In my dream Mort and I were on the top of the peak with them. Earl and Pete have a lot of things named after them in Vail, including Earl's Bowl and Pete's Bowl in Blue Sky Basin.

F is for **Freezing**. Mort and I thought of how we would be freezing when we got out of the hot tub après ski. My dad said après ski meant anything you did after you finished skiing. I waved my hand back and forth through the steam. It was cool to watch it disappear and reappear. Suddenly Mort disappeared! He didn't like being lost in the steam, but I did.

Ella

G is for free **Granola Bars** that are given away at the lift ticket office. We stuffed a lot of them into our pockets. Mort and I thought if we ate enough of them we could tell dad we didn't need to stop for lunch so we'd have more time for skiing! I saved most of my bars for Mort because he was always hungry.

Dylan Dodds

H is for **Half-Pipe** where snowboarders do tricks off the wall. My dad told me the half-pipe was part of the terrain park. "Train park?" I asked. My dad corrected me. "It's called a "terrain park," buddy, not a "train park." I nodded at him and thought to myself, after I learn to snowboard, I am going to get super high up the half-pipe wall!

I is for **Ice Skating** at the Solaris ice rink. It was especially fun to skate there at night. There was a giant statue with lights that moved like an ice skater. My stepmom called it the "Water Tree." "What's a water tree?" I asked. She told me to use my imagination. She twirled and whirled us around over and over and over.

J is for the **Jump** at the pond skimming championships. Mort and I thought the jumpers were AWESOME. I imagined Mort and me trying to make it across the pond too. Yahoo! Afterwards we sat down and padded the snow into balls and took bites out of them. It was like biting into big ice apples. The snow was cold and tasted delicious.

Kyler Weatherred

K is for **Kids Adventure Zones**. There are lots of runs on Vail Mountain created especially for kids. I raced my dad through the trees in Chaos Canyon. He said, "I'm gonna get you," but he couldn't. I was too fast. I cheered, "I won!" as I flew past him.

L is for **Lionshead**. We took the free bus from Vail to Lionshead. Mort and I called it the Magic Bus. You hopped on, and you ended up in another cool place - it was just like magic. Mort and I asked if we could eat some ice cream. My dad didn't understand how we could eat ice cream in the cold. I thought ice cream was better in the cold. Mort agreed.

M is for **Moguls**. Moguls are piles of snow that seem to go on for miles. They were as tall as I. Mort didn't like the moguls. He thought they were too bumpy. I just saw them as another great adventure. I wondered where the moguls went in the summer?

Vail Village
Big Bunn
Valley

Jessie Allen

N is for **Night Sky**. I looked up at the millions and millions and millions of stars. So did Mort. We watched our cold breath go in and out of our mouths like a steam engine. The twinkling of the stars kept us warm.

O is for **Gondola One,** where we started our day on Vail Mountain. Dad said the gondola even had Wi-Fi. I knew what Wi-Fi was, so I asked my dad if I could bring my video games. He said, "No." I didn't mind though because today I was going to learn to snowboard!

P is for **Epic Ski Pass**. Mort loved to show everyone his photo. So did I. The pass was epic because it meant we could ski at so many different mountains whenever we wanted. My stepmom and dad bought them especially for our epic adventures.

epic

Mort

Cole Maurer

Q is for the amazing **Quiet** as the snow fell. I laid down in the snow, so did Mort. We looked up at the sky and let the snowflakes fall on our faces and get caught in our eyelashes. We felt happy. Mort asked me, "Do you want to build a snowman?" I said, "Yes."

Sophie Russell

Moe's Original BAR-B-QUE

R is for **Restaurants**. There are so many restaurants in Vail. Our favorite was Moe's. Mort and I liked how they asked your name and wrote it down. When you get your BBQ, your name is right on your plate. This meant my li'l sis couldn't take my Banana Puddin'!

Annika Love
Iverson

S is for **Sleigh Ride**. Dad thought it would be nice to ride at night. "Clop, clop, clop," was the sound made by the horses' hooves packing down the snow with each stride. It was peaceful. Mort thought so too.

T is for all of the **Tricks** I learned to do. Vroom, zoom I went with my new snowboard. I told my dad I did a back flip off the box. He said, "Really? Probably not buddy." I wasn't sure what "probably not" meant. I figured I would ask him about that after I was finished with my tricks.

U is for staying **Up Late**. My dad took us bowling. Mort was tired from snowboarding and the fresh air. I worked really hard to keep his eyes open. He made it until 9:00 PM. Way, Way, WAY past his bedtime. Woo-hoo!

V is for **Vail Village**. My stepmom says Vail has the best shopping and it looks just like a European ski town. I don't like shopping. Neither does Mort or my li'l sis. So my li'l sis, Mort and I skipped and played while my stepmom and dad shopped. We threw snowballs, jumped in slushy snow and climbed stuff.

W is for **Winter Fun**. Mort and I loved throwing snowballs and playing on the pirate ship at Pirate Ship Playground. Mort pretended to be Captain Hook and threw snow bombs at me. We made pirate faces in the snow with our mittens. My dad said it was time to go inside and get warm, but I didn't feel cold at all. I wanted to keep playing. So did Mort.

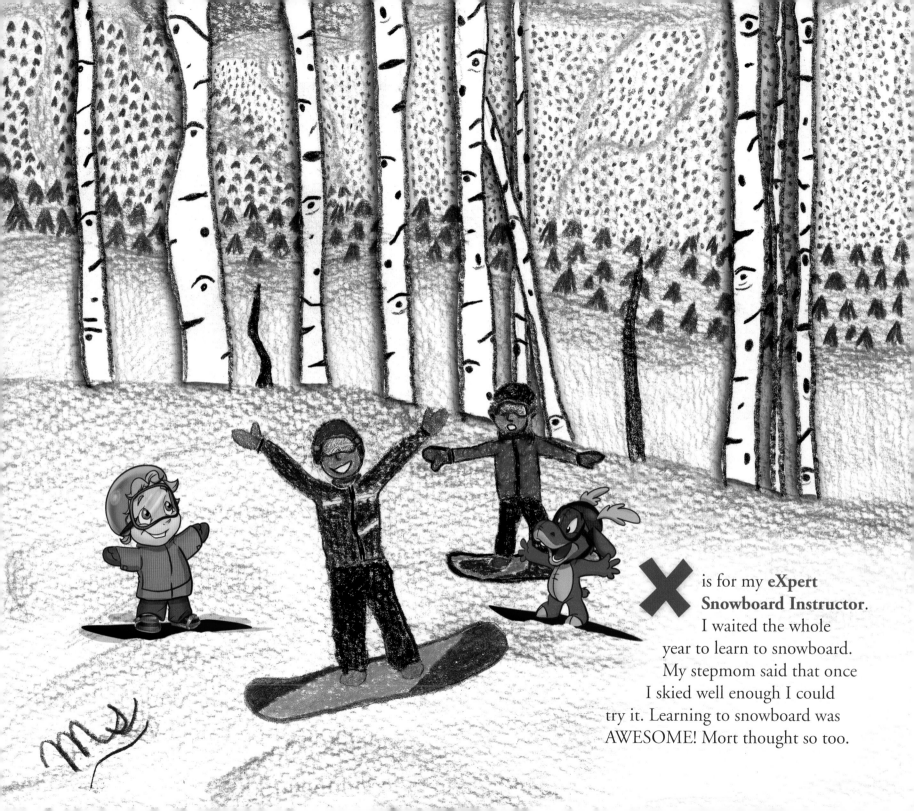

X is for my **eXpert Snowboard Instructor**. I waited the whole year to learn to snowboard. My stepmom said that once I skied well enough I could try it. Learning to snowboard was AWESOME! Mort thought so too.

Y is for **Yodeling**. We saw Helmut Fricker on the streets of Vail, yodeling and playing the alpenhorn. My Dad said Helmut had been in Vail for over 30 years. How long was 30 years? I wasn't sure. Neither was Mort. But it did seem like a REALLY long time!

Z is for **Ziplining**. Even after a day of learning to snowboard, Mort and I were still ready for more adventure. It was SWEET flying through the air, way above the mountain. I was so high I thought I could catch the clouds with my butterfly net. Mort and I can't wait till next year. Our adventure in Vail was EPIC!

MIKA LEITH

Caitlyn Weathers

Mort and I hanging with Mort's friends at the Nature Discovery Center.

Liv Moritz

Nordic skiing ROCKS!

Tommy J.

Colorado Ski Museum

We learned all about the history of skiing and snowboarding at the Colorado Ski and Snowboard Museum.

anthony Blacon

Snowmobiling with Mort was AWESOME!

Outtakes

There was so much more to do in Vail.

See you in Breckenridge
on our next adventure!